# Star Paws

"It's not right," said Neil. "What Jenkins said wasn't true. Prince *saved* Toby's life."

Max buried his face in the spaniel's coat. "It's no good trying to tell them. I've tried millions of times. They won't listen."

"Why not? Why does Jeff listen to Jenkins all the time?" Neil was furious.

Max looked up. "You heard. We're just kids. Nobody listens to us. Jeff thinks Jenkins is the expert on dogs. He's always so busy getting the crew organized, he's blind to everything else. Face it, Neil. Prince won't be in the show any more. And if they won't let Prince do the show, I don't want to do it either."

Titles in the Puppy Patrol series

More Puppy Patrol stories follow soon

# Puppy Patrol
## Star Paws

Jenny Dale

*Illustrated by*
Mick Reid

A Working Partners Book
MACMILLAN CHILDREN'S BOOKS

*Special thanks to Helen McGee*

First published 1997 by Macmillan Children's Books
a division of Macmillan Publishers Limited
25 Eccleston Place, London SW1W 9NF
and Basingstoke

Associated companies throughout the world

Created by Working Partners Limited
London W6 0HE

ISBN 0 330 34909 0

7 9 8

A CIP catalogue record for this book is available from
the British Library.

Typeset in Bookman Old Style
Printed and bound in Great Britain by Mackays of Chatham plc, Kent

# Chapter One

**P**rince raced across the beach, ears back, fur flying in the wind.

"Wait for me!" Zeno yelled. "You can't go without me, Prince!"

The golden cocker spaniel turned his head and barked.

"I am hurrying," Zeno said breathlessly, pounding after the dog.

Behind them, thundering through the shallows, the runners of their sand skimmers spraying sea water, came the Xarcons.

Zeno stumbled on a rock and fell, sprawling on the sand. The skimmers whined on the beach behind him. He looked round. The riders wore black masks which covered all but

1

their mouths. Their cloaks billowed behind them as they sped towards him. There was a humming sound in the air and Zeno turned. In front of him a low, dark shape appeared. Zeno sobbed with exhaustion.

"There it is!" he cried. "There's the tunnel. Go for it, Prince! Leave me. I'm finished."

The dog turned and ran back, pulling on Zeno's sleeve, barking fiercely.

"I can't," Zeno moaned as the humming sand skimmers grew ever closer.

Prince pulled harder until Zeno staggered to his feet and limped towards the dark shape on the sand. The Xarcons were only metres behind. Zeno looked round as the leading rider drew a long thin stick from his belt. The stick flamed red as he raised it, shimmering in reflected light from the water.

Prince dragged at Zeno's trouser leg as the boy staggered, half blinded by the light stick, into the tunnel.

"Yes!" shouted Emily, jumping to her feet. "They've made it. They've got into the time tunnel! Look! The Xarcons didn't catch them."

Neil Parker looked at his sister and smiled.

Emily was nine, two years younger than him. Her dark brown hair was ruffled. Emily had a habit of running her hands through her hair when she was excited. And Emily *always* got excited when she watched *The Time Travellers* on TV.

"Zeno and Prince always get away," said Neil above the programme's closing theme music.

Emily shook her head. "So far," she said. "I thought they'd had it that time."

Mrs Parker reached out and switched the TV off. "I'm surprised that programme doesn't give you nightmares, Emily."

Emily grinned. "It's my favourite," she replied. Then she looked thoughtful. "I wonder where they'll get to next week."

"Somewhere weird and wonderful?" pondered Mrs Parker, smiling.

"The time travellers *always* go to weird and wonderful places!" Neil rolled his eyes.

"You like *The Time Travellers* as well," said Emily accusingly. "You watch it, too."

"I wouldn't let Fudge see it," said Sarah, trying to hum the complicated theme music. "It's scary!"

Sarah was five. She had a hamster called

Fudge and treated the little animal as if it were a person. Sarah was always telling people what Fudge thought of everything.

"It's Prince I like," Neil said. "That dog can do loads of tricks." Neil gave Sam's ears a rub, and the pet black and white Border collie put his head on Neil's knee. "Do you think I could train Sam to be a TV star?"

Mrs Parker laughed and put her head on one side. "How about training yourself to do some homework?"

Neil grinned. "I promised Dad I would give him a hand in the kennels."

"What's that?" said a voice from the door. "Did I hear somebody say 'help'?"

Bob Parker was a tall man with thick dark hair and an infectious smile.

"Oh, Dad, *The Time Travellers* was great tonight," said Emily enthusiastically. "You should have seen it. Zeno and Prince ended up on this really weird planet and the Xarcons tried to capture them."

"But they got away just in time," said Mr Parker.

"How did you know?" said Sarah.

"Magic!" said Mr Parker.

Sarah's eyes grew round. "Wow! You're

clever, Dad. I never know what's going to happen to Prince and Zeno."

Mrs Parker picked up the newspaper. "That reminds me," she said, shuffling through the pages. "There's something in today's paper about your programme, Emily."

Emily jumped up. "What was that?"

"Here it is."

Emily took the paper from her mother. "Oh, wow! Listen to this, Neil. *Popular children's TV series* The Time Travellers *is out on location in the North-West area. The series*

*follows the adventures of a boy and his dog who accidentally get sucked into a space-time tunnel and can't find their way home. Children all over the country follow their adventures every week as they travel backwards and forwards in time and space. So, watch out! They could be recording an episode of the new series somewhere near you!"*

"Maybe they'll do an episode at a boarding kennels." Neil winked at his father.

"Now, what kennels do you have in mind?" Mr Parker said, raising an eyebrow.

Mr and Mrs Parker ran King Street Kennels and rescue centre. The whole family was mad about dogs. They had a dark green Range Rover with the kennels' logo on the side and they were nicknamed the "Puppy Patrol" by everybody around Compton, the busy market town near where they lived.

"If they did an episode at King Street Kennels, Fudge could be in it," Sarah said.

"As if!" mocked Emily. She looked dreamy. "Wouldn't it be great though?"

"I know one thing," Mr Parker said. "I could do with a time tunnel right now."

"Why?" asked Emily.

"So that I could go back a couple of hours and have time for all this work I have to do."

"I was just coming to help." Neil got up from his chair.

"I'll help too," volunteered Emily.

"Promise me you'll do your homework later," Carole Parker insisted.

Neil laughed. "I promise! Come on, Dad, Emily and I are as good as a time tunnel. We'll get the work done in no time."

Bob Parker looked at his older daughter. She was still sitting cross legged on the floor, her chin in her hands, lost in thought.

"Are you coming then, Emily?" he asked.

Emily jumped. "Sorry, Dad. I was just thinking."

"Think outside with a bucket and mop," Mr Parker chuckled.

"Come on, Sam," Neil called.

The Border collie sprang up at the sound of Neil's voice. Sam had been found abandoned as a puppy when Neil was seven. The thin, frightened little dog had been brought to the rescue centre and the Parkers had adopted him as the family pet. Sam had been by Neil's side ever since and he was now fit and healthy. Neil had even taught him lots

7

of agility skills so that he could enter competitions at country shows.

"We had an interesting new arrival today," Bob Parker said as he, Neil and Emily made their way across the courtyard to one of the kennel blocks. Sam ran ahead, tail wagging. He loved visiting the other dogs.

"What breed?" Neil was always interested in new arrivals at King Street.

"It's an Irish wolfhound," Mr Parker said. "His name is Fred and he is absolutely enormous."

"Wow!" said Emily. "We've never had an Irish wolfhound before."

A girl with fair hair tied back in a ponytail came out of the kennel block as they arrived. Sam raced up to her, tail wagging furiously.

"Hey, Sam!" the girl said. "That tail will fall off if you wag it so hard."

"Hi, Kate!" said Neil. "We're just going to have a look at Fred."

Kate McGuire was the King Street kennel maid. She had no animals of her own, but she looked on all the dogs at King Street as her adopted pets.

Kate laughed. "Fred!" she said. "He should

8

be called Giant or Monster or Mr Enormous – not *Fred*."

"He isn't badly behaved, is he?" asked Emily.

Kate shook her head. "Not at all," she replied. "He's terrific – a real gentle giant. I've just been walking him – or rather, he's been walking me!"

Neil grinned. Kate could do anything with dogs. Even the most boisterous dogs calmed down when she was around.

"I'm off," she said, leaning down to give Sam a pat. "See you tomorrow."

Neil waved as Kate collected her bike and rode off. He followed Emily and his dad into the kennel block.

There were two kennel blocks, one on either side of the courtyard. Each contained two rows of ten kennels with a passageway down the middle. Each pen had a basket for the dog to sleep in and a gate to an outside run.

Neil stopped to say hello to some of the dogs. There was a boxer and a Skye terrier in adjoining pens. They both rushed to greet Neil and Sam.

Further down the row, Daisy looked up

and yipped as Neil appeared. Daisy was a little dachshund that Neil had grown very fond of.

"Hi, Daisy," he said, stopping at her pen.

The dachshund waddled across and wagged her tail. Daisy was a little overweight. Neil knew that dachshunds got fat quite easily and he had been very careful not to give her too many dog treats.

"Come and see Fred," Emily called from the far end of the row.

Neil hurried down towards the last pen, with Sam at his heels. He stood lost in admiration. Fred was magnificent.

"He's amazing!" Neil gasped.

Bob Parker lifted the latch and they went in. An enormous dog with a rough grey coat padded over to them and sniffed at Sam. Sam was dwarfed by the huge wolfhound.

"It's OK, Sam," Bob Parker said, gently. "Fred won't eat you."

Sam lifted his muzzle and sniffed at the wolfhound. Then his tail began to wag again. Sam was used to getting on with lots of strange dogs.

"Hi, boy," Neil said, laying his hand on the wolfhound's back, which was level with Neil's waist. Fred looked up at him with liquid brown eyes.

"He's beautiful," Emily breathed.

"*Big* and beautiful, more like," Mr Parker said. "I had to give him an extra-large basket."

Neil ruffled the dog's ears and Fred nuzzled his hand in return.

"Why is he here, Dad?" Neil asked.

"His owner, Bill Grey, has gone away for a few days. We're going to have Fred until midweek."

"Great! I'll take him for a walk tomorrow."

"Hang on tightly," Mr Parker warned. "He's a lot stronger than you."

"A wolfhound is a hunting breed, isn't it?" Neil asked.

Bob Parker nodded. "They were used to hunt stags hundreds of years ago. They were also called war hounds because kings and princes would ride into battle with them."

"You mean like knights in armour?" asked Emily, impressed.

"That sort of thing," said Bob Parker.

"I don't suppose Fred's owner is a king or a prince?" asked Emily.

Mr Parker laughed. "Fred's owner has a butcher's shop in Padsham. Just as well, the way Fred eats!"

"Oh, well, at least Fred is staying at *King* Street," said Neil.

Mr Parker pointed at some buckets nearby. "Come on – time to get to work with those mops."

Neil and Emily helped Mr Parker mop out the kennels and make sure the water bowls were full.

"You two have been a great help," said Bob Parker as they finished. "Now I'll have time for tea before the class tonight."

There were dog training classes at King Street on Wednesday evenings and Sunday mornings. Bob Parker taught all the dogs in the area who needed a little extra help to behave properly. The noisy classes were held in the barn next to the kennel blocks.

"Can I help out?" asked Neil.

"I thought you had homework to do," said Mr Parker.

Neil's face fell. "Oh, yeah. I'd forgotten. I hate homework."

"You'd hate it even more if Mr Hamley gave you detention," Emily said.

Neil grinned. Mr Hamley was a teacher at Meadowbank School in Compton. He had a Dalmatian called Dotty and could be cool sometimes – but was *very* strict about school work.

"Never mind. It's half term next week," Mr Parker reminded him.

"Thank goodness for that," said Emily. "No school for a whole week!"

"OK," said Neil. "I give in. I'll go and hit the books. I just hope Mr Hamley realizes the sacrifice I'm making."

"He won't," said Emily.

Neil shook his head. "Homework! What's the point?"

# Chapter Two

"The point *is*," said Mr Hamley, "that you haven't done your homework, Barry, so you can't go to the audition until you *have* done it. You can do it at lunchtime and, if you finish it, *then* you might have time to catch the audition before it's over."

Barry Pringle's face fell. "I wish I *had* done it now," he said, shuffling past Neil.

Neil turned to his friend, Hasheem.

"Wow! I'm glad I did *my* homework last night."

Hasheem shook his head. "Poor Barry," he said as the boy slouched back to his seat, head down. "He must be really disappointed."

14

Neil's class was buzzing with excitement after Mr Hamley's announcement. Prince Productions, the TV company that made *The Time Travellers*, was recording an episode in nearby Padsham – and they were looking for additional children to be involved in some of the crowd scenes. There were going to be auditions at lunchtime in *their* school hall.

"Can you believe it?" said Hasheem, leaning across his desk towards Neil. "This could be the start of my movie career."

"Dream on!" said Neil. "You'll only be in the background. Even if you *do* get picked, nobody will recognize you."

"Says who?" said Hasheem. "Haven't you ever heard of the star of the show breaking his leg and suddenly, from out of nowhere, the director says – 'Hasheem! This is your big moment!' "

"If you don't get on with your work, *you* won't be going to the auditions either," said a voice.

Hasheem looked up. "Uh-oh! Sorry, Mr Hamley," he muttered.

Neil bent over his workbook. It was really hard to concentrate. He kept thinking about

15

the auditions. Imagine getting a part in *The Time Travellers*!

It seemed ages before lunchtime finally came. Neil bumped into his best friend, Chris Wilson, outside the school hall.

"Are you going to audition?" Neil asked Chris.

"You bet. I reckon everybody will want to."

Chris was right. The school hall was full. Neil, Chris and Hasheem crammed themselves in at the back. The headmaster was up on the stage with Mrs Potter, the drama teacher. There were two men standing beside them. One was youngish and fair. The other was older, with receding dark hair, and looked a bit nervous.

Slightly behind them was a dark-haired boy with a dog. Neil recognized the young star who played Zeno in *The Time Travellers*. He was about the same age as Neil but didn't look very happy. Neil could see the dog sitting quietly at the boy's feet.

"It's Prince!" he whispered, gazing at the golden cocker spaniel.

Prince sat watching all the people in the hall with interest. He didn't seem the least bit bothered by the noise. The spaniel had silky ears, furry feet and a long feathery tail. To Neil's expert eye, he looked a perfect specimen of his breed.

"Attention, please!" said the headmaster, and the pupils fell silent.

"I want to introduce Mr Mason, Mr Jenkins and Max," the headmaster went on. "They've come along this morning to audition potential supporting artistes for an episode of *The Time Travellers* which they'll be recording this weekend."

"*Supporting artistes*?" said Hasheem, looking confused.

"'Extras' to you," whispered Chris.

"Now, I know you are all interested," continued the headmaster, "so let's hear more about it, shall we?"

He stepped aside and the fair-haired man walked forward.

"Hello, everybody. I'm Brian Mason, the director of the show. That means I'm responsible for what you see on your TV screens when you watch *The Time Travellers*. I deal with the recording of the programme and also the casting of the characters. That's why I'm here today. I thought it would also be an idea to bring along Mr Jenkins, Max, and, of course, Prince. You'll be seeing them all again on Saturday if you are lucky enough to be chosen.

"The episode we'll be recording is set in medieval times and I'm looking for some people to be in the large crowd scenes we have planned."

"Wow! Knights in armour!" Chris said. "Do you think they'll give us swords?"

"We're going to be shooting mainly around Padsham Castle," Brian Mason went on. "The story is that Zeno and Prince help the rightful owner of the castle to get it back from his evil brother. Padsham is perfect for us, so we need people who can get there easily."

"Excellent," whispered Neil to Hasheem. "The castle is just a bike ride away."

"We also need people who've got a lot of patience," said Mr Mason, smiling. "You probably won't believe me, but recording TV programmes is mostly about standing around – and all too often when we're taping outside, it means standing around in the rain."

"Patience?" said Chris. "That rules you out, Hasheem."

Mr Mason was speaking again. "One more

thing. If you're chosen as an extra you'll need to make sure an adult can come to the set with you. If we use anybody under the age of sixteen we need a chaperone to be officially responsible for them at all times. It's the law, I'm afraid."

"A chaperone!" said Hasheem. "What about my street cred?"

"You'll have to put up with it," said Chris. "You heard what the man said."

"It's for the sake of your art," said Neil, grinning.

Hasheem laughed. "Oh, well, in that case, I don't mind."

"Listen!" Neil whispered. "He's telling us what we have to do."

"We're going to ask you to walk around the room first," Brian Mason went on. "If I tap you on the shoulder, please go to the side of the room and stay there."

"That's all?" said Chris. "It doesn't sound like much of an audition."

"Tut, tut. Have *patience*," said Hasheem, and Chris gave him a thump.

"Look! There's Barry," said Neil. "He must have done that homework in double-quick time."

Barry gave them a wave. His face was flushed and his hair stood on end.

"Made it!" he gasped as he came to stand beside them.

Mrs Potter stepped forward and clapped her hands. "Just start walking around. Be yourselves – act normally."

Neil and Chris looked at each other. "OK, so we walk," said Neil as the whole crowd moved forward.

"I feel like an idiot," grumbled Chris.

"That's what Mrs Potter said," Hasheem chipped in. "Just act normal."

The director jumped down from the stage and began to walk amongst them. Neil was still watching Prince. The man called Jenkins turned round to say something to Max and the dog flinched and shrank back. Max looked down, his hand going to Prince's head. The dog settled down, but Neil saw the boy's face tighten as he replied to Mr Jenkins.

Neil felt a tap on his shoulder and turned in time to see Brian Mason heading off into the crowd. Neil walked towards the side of the room, head down. Emily and her friend, Julie Baker, were there already.

"So, you got the elbow too?" said Emily, gloomily.

Neil nodded and leaned back against the wall. "I was watching Prince," he sighed, kicking the wall with his heel. "I should have concentrated on walking."

"I'm sorry you lost out too, Neil." Julie looked as sad as he felt. Then she brightened a little as she gazed across the hall. "Isn't Prince gorgeous, though? He reminds me of Ben."

Ben was Julie's Old English sheepdog.

"How can he remind you of Ben?" Neil

said, amazed. "They're completely different breeds!"

"I know what Julie means." Emily looked thoughtful. "Prince is so friendly looking, like Ben." Her mouth turned down. "I'd have loved to have been chosen."

Neil forgot his own disappointment and tried to cheer her up. "Never mind. At least you've seen Prince. And we can always go and watch."

Emily smiled. "Do you think Max would give me his autograph?"

Neil looked at the boy on the stage. He had his hand on Prince's neck. "Why not?" he said. "He seems all right – not too stuck-up or anything. He looks as if he likes Prince."

Hasheem and Chris came wandering up.

"Bang goes my movie career," said Hasheem. "Maybe I should have done one of my funny walks."

"Barry is still in the running," Neil said. "Lucky old Barry!"

"They must need an awful lot of extras," Chris said. "Look! Mr Mason has finished eliminating people."

Neil looked around. There were about twenty boys and girls lining the walls.

"What did we do that was so bad?" groaned Hasheem. "I learned to walk years ago. I thought I was quite good at it."

Mrs Potter clapped her hands for silence.

"Thank you all so much," she said. "If the people at the side of the room could just stay there, Mr Mason has some more selecting to do. The rest of you can go – I do hope you aren't too disappointed at not being picked."

Neil's mouth dropped open.

"*Yes!*" said Hasheem, punching the air. "We *were* selected."

They watched as everybody else filed out of the hall.

"Hard luck, Barry," Neil said as the other boy passed him.

Barry grinned. "At least I got to try."

Brian Mason smiled at the pupils who were left.

"Now I want to try a few things with you," he said. "I'm going to give you instructions and I want you to obey them as well as you can."

They had to do all sorts of things – form up in twos, in fives, run the length of the hall, fall down, jump up, cheer and, best of all, pretend they were attacking a castle wall.

"Great!" said the director from the stage when they had finished shouting battle cries at the tops of their voices. "There's a scene in the episode where the local peasants join forces with Zeno and Prince and attack the castle. That looked terrific."

"Peasants," said Chris softly. "No chance of a sword then?"

"Mrs Potter and I have made some notes," the director went on. "We'll need fifteen extras from this group and the names will go up on the noticeboard this afternoon. Thank you all very much for coming."

"I can't stand the suspense," said Hasheem. "I won't be able to work this afternoon."

"So what's new?" said Neil, grinning.

Emily was almost dancing beside him. "I'm going to ask for Max's autograph," she said, pulling a piece of paper and a pencil out of her pocket.

Neil watched as Brian Mason and Mrs Potter came down the steps from the stage, chatting together. Max was behind them with Prince.

24

"Excuse me," Emily said shyly, holding out the pencil and paper. "Can I have your autograph?

Max looked round and smiled. "Sure," he said. "What do you want me to put?"

Emily and Max went into a huddle. Neil could hear Emily dictating a message to Max. Neil bent down and held out his hand, palm face up, to Prince. The cocker spaniel sniffed delicately, then licked his hand.

Neil smiled and crouched down, stroking Prince's silky coat, tickling him under the chin. Prince's eyes closed and he held his head up for more.

"What do you think you're doing?" said a voice.

Neil looked up. It was Mr Jenkins.

"I was just saying hello," Neil replied.

The man grunted. "That's a valuable dog. Don't you go getting him upset. We can't have all you kids annoying him."

Neil flushed. "I wouldn't annoy him," he muttered. "And he *isn't* upset."

"What do you call that then, eh?" said Jenkins, pointing at the dog.

Neil looked down. Prince had backed off and Neil thought he was cowering a little.

"He was OK a moment ago," Neil said, surprised.

Mr Jenkins grunted again. "Temperamental, that's what he is. He's spoilt rotten, that dog."

The man stomped away, tugging Prince's lead. The dog followed him warily. Neil looked round and saw Max staring after him, his eyes stormy.

"I didn't do anything," Neil said, bewildered.

Max looked at him. For a moment Neil thought he was going to say something. Then he turned away and walked after the others.

"Well!" said Hasheem. "That wasn't very friendly, was it?"

"And he was so nice about the autograph," Emily commented. "I wonder what annoyed him."

Julie frowned. "Maybe he didn't like you petting Prince."

Neil bit his lip. "As if I would do anything to upset a dog."

Emily put her hand on his arm. "We know you wouldn't," she said. "But strangers might not realize that. Cheer up, Neil. If you get chosen as an extra you'll be able to show Max you aren't like that."

"*If*," said Neil. "From the way Max looked at me, I don't think he would want me anywhere near him or Prince."

# Chapter Three

Neil, Chris and Hasheem hurried out of class at the end of lessons but Emily was still at the noticeboard before them.

"We're in!" she yelled, her face shining.

"What? All of us?" Chris couldn't believe it.

Julie clenched her fist. "Me too! I'm so excited. Isn't it great?"

Neil looked at the list. It really *was* true. His name *was* there.

"We've got to be at Padsham Castle on Saturday morning at seven o'clock," he said, reading the notice. "They'll need us Sunday too."

"Seven!" groaned Hasheem. "That's the middle of the night!"

"It also says breakfast and lunch will be provided," Neil went on.

Hasheem looked a bit more cheerful.

"I'm really excited," laughed Emily, dancing around. "Just think! We'll be on TV. Do you think we'll get costumes?"

"We'll need to get an adult to come with us," Julie reminded them.

"I'll ask Mum," Neil said.

Hasheem pulled a notebook out of his pocket and started scribbling in it.

"What are you doing?" Julie asked.

Hasheem looked surprised. "Practising my autograph, of course!"

Chris gave him a shove. "Don't be daft. We're only extras."

"Everybody has to start somewhere," Hasheem said, seriously. "This could be my big break."

Chris laughed. "Oh, sure. *Hasheem, star of stage and screen.*"

"It's going to be great seeing Prince at work," said Neil, as they made their way out of school. "He's a really clever dog. Very well trained. Nothing seemed to bother him in the hall today."

"Except that Jenkins man," Chris chipped in.

Neil agreed. He suspected there was something more to Jenkins' aggressive manner than a lack of personality, but he couldn't think what.

Emily interrupted his thoughts. "Just wait till we tell Mum and Dad we're going to be on TV!"

"I can't wait till Saturday," Hasheem whooped, as they were all swept out of the school gates by the rush of people. "Fame and fortune, here I come!"

"Look at all the people!" Neil said breathlessly as Mrs Parker drove the Range Rover through the gates of Padsham Castle on Saturday morning. She wiped her brow with one hand. It was very hot.

"Where's Prince?" Sarah piped up.

"Inside, somewhere cool, if he has any sense," Emily said.

Even though it was so early in the morning, the whole of the lawn in front of the castle was already crowded with people. Some of them were running around with bits of paper and complicated-looking equipment.

Everyone seemed hot and bothered. There were also a number of big blue vans parked in the castle grounds with *Prince Productions* written on the side. The air felt close and sticky.

"I'd love a cool drink," said Neil.

Emily nodded. The heat had been building up all week and some of the dogs at King Street had been restless because of it.

"That looks like a catering van over there," said Emily. "Maybe we could buy some cans."

Mrs Parker manoeuvred the Range Rover into a parking space. "Where did you say you would meet the others?" she asked.

"By the drawbridge," Emily replied. "It's really good of you to chaperone us, Mum."

Carole Parker laughed. "As if I had any choice once Sarah heard about it!"

Sarah jiggled up and down in her seat. "I wish *I* could be an extra."

"You're too young," said Mrs Parker. "But, to make up for it, I'll buy you a drink, too. Come on. We'll meet you at the drawbridge, Neil."

Neil and Emily wove their way through the crowds.

"There's Mrs Jones," said Emily, waving at

a grey-haired lady with a dog who was standing by the drawbridge in front of the castle. "I bet she's thrilled by all this excitement!"

Mrs Jones waved back and Toby, her little wire-haired terrier, barked a welcome. Toby was ten and came to King Street to board from time to time. He was a very lively little dog for his age and always up to mischief.

Neil sighed. "I wish I had been able to bring Sam. I feel really bad about leaving him behind."

"He's got all the other dogs at King Street to keep him company," Emily said. "Oh, look, Neil! Doesn't the castle look terrific?"

Padsham Castle wasn't really that old. It had been built about a hundred years ago by an eccentric but very rich local man who thought it would be a good idea to live in a castle. But it *looked* really old – apart from the fact that it was in pretty good condition. It had turrets and slit windows and even a drawbridge in front of the huge main door.

The castle had been turned into a local history museum, and Meadowbank School sometimes went on trips there. Maggie Jones lived in a cottage in the grounds. She was the caretaker and sold tickets for the museum, as well as generally keeping an eye on the place.

"These people can't *all* be extras," said Emily, looking around in amazement.

Neil shook his head. "I reckon a lot of people have come to watch." He smiled. "There's Chris!"

Chris was walking towards Mrs Jones. Toby jumped up at him with a stick in his mouth.

Neil laughed. "Poor Toby. Mrs Jones hasn't got time to play with him today."

"Loads of people have come to watch the programme being made, haven't they?" Chris said, eagerly looking around. "Mrs Jones says she's never had so many visitors to the castle."

"It's true," Mrs Jones said. "Twenty years I've been caretaker here and I've never seen the like of it. And the vans! Huge great things parked all over the place. Wires trailing everywhere, people shouting, cameras. They've even got a mobile canteen!"

"We saw it," said Neil. "Mum's already gone to get us some drinks."

"It's so hot," Emily groaned.

"Certainly is," said Chris. "I could do with a drink, too. See you in a few minutes." He walked off in the direction of the catering van.

Mrs Jones looked up at the sky. "This glorious weather has to break soon. Toby has been very jumpy these last few days."

"So have some of the dogs at King Street," Neil agreed. "One was spinning round in circles trying to catch her own tail! I think she was a bit uncomfortable in the heat." He bent down to Toby. "Poor Toby! How are you coping, boy?"

The little wire-haired terrier wagged his stumpy tail and dropped his stick at Neil's feet.

"OK," Neil said. "I'll throw it for you."

He picked up the stick and looked around. "There's a clear space over by the castle wall. Is it all right if I give Toby a quick run, Mrs Jones?"

Mrs Jones looked relieved. "That would be good of you," she said, unclipping Toby's lead. "I've been so busy this morning I haven't had time – he loves chasing sticks."

"Come on, Toby," Neil called, breaking into a run.

Toby barked excitedly and chased after him across the castle drive. Out of the corner of his eye Neil saw a long black car sweep in through the gates of the castle. There was an excited babble of voices from the crowd at the gates. Toby barked and Neil laughed.

"OK," he said. "Don't worry. I haven't forgotten our game."

He threw the stick and the little dog raced after it. Just at that moment the black car stopped at the drawbridge and Max got out, followed by Mr Jenkins. Then Prince jumped out of the car.

Toby raced back to Neil with the stick, and Neil threw it towards the car. It was too late before Neil realized what he had done. Suddenly Prince was off, racing towards the stick. Toby stopped, barked, and raced on.

"Prince!" Max shouted. "Come back!"

Mr Jenkins swung round and saw Neil.

"Get that dog out of here!" he yelled.

Neil gulped. Toby was almost on the stick – so was Prince. Prince got to it first and raced off with it. Toby, barking madly, followed at his heels. Prince turned briefly, swerved and scampered off in the other direction – towards Neil. Mr Jenkins started running towards him too, shouting as he went.

Neil made a dive for Prince as the dog hurtled past him, but Prince was too quick. The golden cocker spaniel swerved, his long feathery tail flowing behind him, just as Toby caught up. Neil found himself clutching Toby instead of Prince. He grabbed hold of Toby's collar and hung on. Then he gathered up the little dog into his arms.

"One down, one to go," he said.

"I'll get Prince," shouted a voice, and Neil spun round.

Max was racing across the lawn towards the cocker spaniel, cornering him in an angle of the castle wall. Prince stopped and turned, looking at Max.

"Here, boy," Max said softly. "Give me the stick."

Prince began to walk towards Max, tail wagging.

"What the devil do you think you're doing?" roared a voice in Neil's ear. Neil felt Toby quiver in his arms. Then he saw a flash of golden fur and Prince was off again.

Max whirled round. "You've scared him!" he said, angrily.

"Rubbish," said Mr Jenkins. "He just can't behave properly."

Max bit his lip. Neil could see he was really upset.

"He does what *I* tell him," Max muttered.

"That's because you're always giving him treats," said Jenkins. "What he needs is a bit of discipline."

"Don't you touch him," Max said through gritted teeth.

"I'm his trainer," retorted the man. "I should know."

Max looked furious. "If you lay a finger on him, I'll tell Brian."

Mr Jenkins hesitated and his eyes shifted nervously. "Who said anything about laying a finger on him? Don't you go telling stories you can't prove. And, if you're so good with him, you get him back."

Neil watched as Mr Jenkins turned on his heel and walked off. "Wow!" he said to Max. "Is that *really* Prince's trainer?"

Max put his fingers between his lips and whistled. There was a rustle from a clump of bushes and Prince appeared, the stick still in his mouth. Max knelt down, arms out, and Prince began to race towards him.

"It's his *temporary* trainer," Max said. "The real one is ill and she won't be coming back for another two weeks."

Toby squirmed in Neil's arms, but Neil held on tight. "Oh no you don't," he told the little dog. "We've already got Max and Prince into enough trouble."

Max turned briefly and smiled. "It wasn't your fault. Jenkins doesn't like Prince. Sometimes you'd think he doesn't even like dogs!"

"Then why is he a dog trainer?" Neil asked.

Max didn't reply. Prince came galloping up and threw himself at the boy. Boy and dog fell in a heap, rolling over and over on the grass. The stick was forgotten as Prince and Max greeted each other. Jenkins might not like Prince very much, but one thing was certain. Max did. Max loved Prince.

# Chapter Four

"Neil!" Chris yelled, running up with his hands full of cans of Coke. "They want us over at the costume van."

Julie and Hasheem were close behind him. They had drinks too.

"Your mum and Sarah are just coming," Julie said to Emily. "Hi, Mrs Jones."

"We didn't even have to pay for the Coke!" said Hasheem, astonished. "I really like this acting lark."

"Look what I found," said Julie, excitedly, waving a thick wodge of coloured paper in the air.

"It's a script," Neil marvelled. "Let's have a look."

They all peered over Julie's shoulder as she leafed through the script.

"Baron Dredmore is the baddie," said Julie. "He takes over Sir Gareth Norton's castle – that's his brother – and Zeno and Prince arrive through the time tunnel. Then Baron Dredmore captures Prince."

"What happens then?" asked Hasheem.

Julie flicked over another few pages. "Oh, this is where we come in. Zeno gets all the villagers organized to storm the castle and rescue Prince and Lady Genevieve."

"Who's she?" asked Hasheem.

"Baron Dredmore has locked her in the tower," said Julie. "I think she's Sir Gareth's girlfriend."

"Knights didn't have girlfriends in those days," Emily said.

"So what did they have?" Julie asked.

Emily shrugged. "Something a lot more posh than girlfriends."

"Never mind that," said Chris, hurriedly. "We've got to go and get ready."

He pointed towards one of the big blue vans parked in a roped-off area just inside the castle walls. Several men in jeans and T-shirts were carrying cameras and light stands across the lawn and into the castle. Another two were herding a lot of spectators behind a roped-off area, well out of the way of the equipment, ready for the start of recording.

Carole Parker and Sarah arrived just as Neil handed Toby back to Mrs Jones.

"Why don't you come over to the cottage for a cup of tea?" Mrs Jones said to Carole Parker.

"I'd love that, Maggie," Mrs Parker said.

"And I can play with Toby!" Sarah looked excitedly at the little dog.

"If you need me, you'll know where I am," Mrs Parker told Neil.

Neil nodded. "See you later." Toby barked and Neil laughed. "You too, Toby."

"Good luck," said Mrs Jones. "What is it they say to actors? Break a leg!"

Julie snapped the ring-pull of her can and took a long drink. Her fringe was sticking to her forehead with the heat.

"That's better," she gasped. "I'm *so* hot! And we've still got to get costumes. I hope they aren't too heavy."

Emily began to drag Neil towards the

castle gates. "And there's make-up. Mine will run with this heat."

Neil looked with interest at the van as they approached. A side door was open and inside was a rail with costumes hanging from it. A worried-looking woman with untidy hair and glasses on the end of her nose was lining up the extras.

"That must be the wardrobe mistress," said Julie. "Isn't it exciting?"

"Smallest at the front," the wardrobe mistress told them. "Now, let me see, I want eleven peasants, one page boy, two milkmaids and a shepherd's boy."

"Does the shepherd's boy have a dog?" Neil asked before he could help himself.

The woman looked at him over the top of her glasses. "No, but you'll do. Here's your costume. You'll get a shepherd's crook over there." She took a hanger with a pair of baggy trousers, a loose shirt and a leather jerkin off the rail and handed it to Neil.

"Poor you!" said Chris. "That jerkin looks heavy."

Neil sighed. "Where do I change?" he asked.

The woman looked at his jeans and

T-shirt. "There's a dressing caravan for all the extras to change in," she said. "But your costume will easily go on over the clothes you're wearing, if you like."

"No way! I'd rather take them off, thank you. I'm boiling."

"No star dressing room for you," Hasheem joked.

The woman grabbed him. "You'll make a great page boy," she said. "Here, put these on."

Hasheem looked in disbelief at the short tunic, the leggings and the hat with a feather in it.

"I can't wear *that*," he said, in disgust.

"You want to be on TV, don't you?" the woman said, her hands on her hips.

Hasheem nodded.

"Then that's what you wear. Next!"

Chris was still hooting with laughter at Hasheem when the woman grabbed him. "You're a peasant," she announced briskly.

"Thanks a bundle," sighed Chris, taking a heap of what looked like rags from her.

When Hasheem and Chris came out of the extras' dressing caravan, Neil was already at Make-up. His costume had fitted perfectly.

The make-up girl slapped some cream on his face and rubbed it in. Then she dipped her fingers in a pot of grey gunge and spread some over his hands and face.

"Yuck!" said Neil. "What's that for?"

"To make you look as if you haven't washed for a week," the girl said, smiling. "Boys in the Middle Ages didn't have showers, you know."

"What I want to know," said Emily, coming

up to them, "is why couldn't I be a princess instead of a peasant?"

Julie was with her. She had a white apron over a long blue dress and she was carrying a wooden bucket.

Neil looked her up and down. "You don't look too bad."

Julie grimaced. "I'm a milkmaid."

"You're lucky then," said the make-up girl. "You don't have to look dirty. Line up over there and you'll get your instructions."

"Over there" was in front of the drawbridge, well away from the spectators. A crowd of people had gathered round the edge of the roped-off area, pointing and smiling in their direction.

Emily joined Neil and the others, looking excited. "We've just seen Max. He's got a chaperone all to himself."

"She's called Suzie and she has to be on set when Max is working," added Julie. "She's really nice."

"Look, there she is, going into the castle with Max," Emily said, pointing.

Neil looked. Max was with a tall dark-haired woman. She and Max looked as if they were sharing a joke.

Brian Mason was standing on the drawbridge with a youngish-looking man who had bright red hair and wore gold-rimmed glasses.

"Gather round," Brian said to the extras.

Everybody shuffled into place while Brian introduced the man beside him.

"This is Jeff Calton. He's the producer of the series and he's always doing ten things at once! Jeff's going to quickly explain what we want you to do today."

Jeff peered at the group through his glasses and smiled. "You all look great. And I know you're going to do your best for us and for *The Time Travellers*. I hope you're all fans."

Everybody nodded.

"Great," Jeff went on. "I'm the guy in charge of this whole operation here today, and it's important that everything goes without a hitch. We always like to use fans as extras because they take their work seriously. If there are any problems, let me know at once. Problems cost time and money and the sooner we solve them, the better for everybody. Understood?"

There were more nods all round. Neil was impressed.

"Good," said Jeff. "Now, we're going to be doing all of the scenes set inside the castle today." He looked up at the sky. "It's a bit overcast for exterior shots and, besides, it'll be cooler inside."

Everybody sighed with relief. Neil looked up. The sky was already heavy with heat and the light wasn't very good.

Brian Mason took over and began to describe how the first shot was going to work. "The first scene we're going to shoot this morning is just after Zeno creeps into the castle to rescue Prince, who has been kidnapped by Baron Dredmore. You lot are helping him because you all hate Baron Dredmore and want to restore the castle to its rightful owner, Sir Gareth Norton. Baron Dredmore catches Zeno, then Sir Gareth arrives and leads you all into the castle. We're going to shoot the scene from inside the great hall. We'll get a shot through the doorway of Sir Gareth jumping off his horse, so all you have to do is come in after him, waving your hands in the air and shouting." The director looked round his cast of young villagers. "Any questions?"

"What do we shout?" asked Hasheem.

Jeff Calton smiled. "Let's leave that to your imagination and see how it goes. But nothing rude."

"Let's try it a couple of times before we go for a take," Brian said, giving a signal to the production crew behind them.

Neil grinned. This was going to be great.

"Wow!" gasped Chris. "Look at that!"

Neil looked round. Max was walking towards them with two other actors and Prince. One of the actors was dressed all in black and looked really frightening. Neil knew that had to be Baron Dredmore. The other one was riding a beautiful chestnut horse with a kind of skirt under its saddle. He was carrying a shield and wearing armour and a helmet with a huge white plume on top of it. He must be Sir Gareth. There was a man wearing riding boots walking by the horse's side.

"I suppose that's the horse trainer," Emily guessed. "Don't the knights look terrific?"

Neil laughed. "Sir Gareth should have a Fred with him."

"What's a Fred?" said a voice behind him.

Neil looked round. It was Jeff. "Oh," Neil muttered, embarrassed. "Sorry! I didn't know you were there."

"So what *is* a Fred?" Jeff asked again.

"Fred is a dog," Neil said. "Actually, he's an Irish wolfhound. He's staying at our kennels at the moment and my dad was telling me that in the olden days kings and princes and barons and people like that used to have wolfhounds."

Jeff's eyes lit up behind his glasses. "A sort of war hound, then. Of course! I never thought of that."

"Places, everybody!" Brian shouted as Max and the two men crossed the drawbridge. "Let's get this show on the road."

Fifteen minutes later the cameras were ready to record the scene.

"This is great," Emily said as they trooped out of the castle for the third time. "But it's just as well they've cleared all the exhibits out of the great hall, with all of us rushing about."

"Not all of them," Julie pointed out. "They've still got that big chair in there. It looks like a throne now that it's all draped with velvet and stuff. It's really cool."

"I love all the shouting," Neil said. "*Down with Baron Dredmore!*"

"Poor Hasheem doesn't get to do any shouting," Chris said. "All he has to do is stand behind that throne thing."

Neil looked up at the sky. "At least he's out of the rain." The first drops were beginning to fall. "Maybe a good downpour will clear the air."

"OK, on my cue – go! And, remember, don't look at the camera," called the director from the drawbridge.

Sir Gareth trotted across the drawbridge on his horse, flung himself from the saddle and ran into the castle. The villagers followed, shouting enthusiastically.

Neil burst through the castle door with Chris and Julie beside him. Max was standing in front of the huge chair, which had a red velvet cushion on it. Baron Dredmore had Prince by the collar in one hand and his sword in the other.

"No, you don't!" yelled Max and made a lunge for Baron Dredmore's sword.

Baron Dredmore raised his sword – and Sir Gareth raced across the floor, knocking it from his hand. The crowd cheered. Baron Dredmore let go of Prince and turned to face Sir Gareth. Prince scampered off.

"Cut!" shouted Brian.

Neil looked round. "Look at Prince!"

The cocker spaniel was sitting on the big chair in the centre of the hall, looking as if he belonged there.

"No wonder he's called Prince," Chris said, chuckling. "That chair really does look like a throne."

Max heard him and turned, laughing. Then Jenkins, the trainer, walked over to the chair and took hold of Prince's collar. Prince barked and refused to budge.

"He likes it there," Julie said, smiling.

Jenkins turned to her. "That dog is spoilt. He won't do a thing he's told."

Jeff Calton walked over, eager to get proceedings started again as soon as possible. He took his glasses off and polished them on his T-shirt. He looked worried. "You aren't having trouble with him again, are you, Harry?"

Harry Jenkins pursed his mouth. "The dog is temperamental. He's unmanageable sometimes."

Max moved forward. "No, he isn't. *You* just don't know how to handle him."

Jeff looked at Max. "I haven't got time for

this, Max. I've told you about this before. Mr Jenkins is the trainer around here. Let's not forget that, eh?" The producer looked stressed.

Max bit his lip. Neil felt really sorry for him. But, he thought, performing dogs had to do what the trainer told them. Maybe Prince *was* getting a bit unruly.

"I might have another job for you, Harry," Jeff told Jenkins. "I'm thinking about getting a wolfhound in on some of the scenes with Sir Gareth."

"A wolfhound!" grumbled Jenkins, shaking his head. "You'd better be careful there. Wolfhounds can be dangerous things."

"Can they?" said Jeff, looking concerned. "I didn't know that. Maybe it isn't such a good idea after all." He looked round and smiled at Neil. "It *was* only an idea."

Neil's mouth dropped open in surprise.

"He took you seriously!" Chris whispered to him.

But Neil wasn't listening. Jenkins was looking at him and the expression on his face wasn't pleasant.

Neil's mind raced. Why was the trainer looking at him like that? Then he knew.

Jenkins was angry because he realized Neil had suggested having a wolfhound in the programme. Neil looked at the trainer. What had he said about wolfhounds? That they were dangerous? Rubbish! Wolfhounds were the gentlest dogs you could find. But they *were* big. What was the matter with Jenkins? A dog trainer that was scared of dogs? Jeff seemed too busy to notice what was going on right in front of him. Neil shook his head. But what on earth *was* going on?

# Chapter Five

"You nearly got a part in *The Time Travellers* today, Fred," Neil said to the Irish wolfhound later that evening.

"What's that?" asked Mr Parker.

Neil was making the evening rounds of the kennels with his father, finishing up with Fred. He could hear the rain drumming on the roof. It had been raining steadily since late afternoon.

"The producer heard me saying that Sir Gareth should have a wolfhound," Neil explained. "He thought it was a great idea at first."

"But he changed his mind?" his dad asked.

Neil knelt down and ruffled Fred's ears. The big dog put a paw on Neil's shoulder and wagged his tail.

"Mr Jenkins, the trainer, said wolfhounds were too fierce." Neil looked into Fred's liquid eyes. "But that isn't true, is it, Fred? You're as soft as putty."

"It certainly isn't true," said Mr Parker, puzzled. "What an odd thing for a trainer to say."

Neil shrugged. "Max says Mr Jenkins doesn't like dogs. Weird or what?"

He stood up, dislodging Fred's paw. The wolfhound nuzzled his hand.

Neil frowned. "The producer just doesn't see it, either. He's always too wrapped up in other things when he's on the set. I'd like to find out more."

"Time to go, anyway," Mr Parker said.

Neil gave Fred a final pat and latched the door of the pen. He followed his father out of the kennel block.

"You know, Dad, Mr Jenkins does seem a bit nervous – even around Prince."

Mr Parker shook his head. "That's just about the worse thing to be when you're handling dogs. Unless Prince *has* shown signs of bad temper. Has he ever snapped at anybody?"

Neil shook his head. "Not that I've seen. But Prince isn't very good at doing what Mr Jenkins tells him."

"Mmm," said his dad, thoughtfully. "It might just be that they don't get on."

"Maybe."

"You don't sound convinced."

"I'm not. And I'm going to keep an eye on Mr Jenkins. I don't think it's Prince's fault that they don't get on – *if* that's what's wrong."

Bob Parker laughed. "You *never* blame the dog, Neil."

Neil laughed back. He felt better. "I wonder where I got *that* idea from!"

As they ran through the rain to the house, Neil thought of his dad's favourite saying – if a dog has a problem, look at the owner. Or, in this case, the trainer. Then another thought occurred to him. Who *was* Prince's owner?

Neil got a chance to ask that question next morning back at the castle. Chris's mum was acting as chaperone that day and was having a great time looking round the set. Neil had a couple of minutes before he was needed on set, and left the others to search for Max.

He found the young actor still in Make-up, and peered into the caravan. "Hi, Max. Not disturbing you, am I?"

Max turned round in his seat in front of a large mirror, and smiled. "No way. Come on in. Excuse me not looking at you while we talk, though – I'm still getting the gunge caked on!"

Neil clambered in and sat down on an upturned basket behind Max's chair. "It's nothing, really. I was just wondering about Prince."

"Great, isn't he? What about him?"

"Do you own him?"

Max sighed. "I wish he *were* my dog. Prince is from an agency. They supply the other animals we use too. I suppose the agency owns him."

Neil studied Max for a moment. The young actor wasn't much different to himself. A bit taller, perhaps, and his hair was darker, but it was clear that, like him, Max loved dogs and was very attached to Prince. Neil hoped he hadn't asked something that had upset him. "I wish he was yours too," Neil said, nodding. "Prince does everything you tell him."

Their conversation was interrupted by a shout from just outside the doorway. "Places, everybody!" It was Brian Mason. "Let's try and get these outside shots done before the rain comes on again. We've got a lot to do today."

"Come on, Max," said a voice behind Neil.

He looked round. It was Suzie, Max's chaperone. She smiled at Neil. "Enjoying yourself?" she asked.

Neil nodded enthusiastically. "It's terrific, thanks. We're all loving it."

Suzie smiled again and Neil watched her

and Max walk off towards the first location. Mr Jenkins might be a problem for Max, but Suzie was a definite bonus!

Neil followed them for a moment and then saw Mrs Wilson again, standing behind one of the cameras, watching all the activity. He waved at her and she smiled back.

There weren't nearly so many spectators this morning. It had rained all night and the grass was wet and slippery underfoot. But the rain hadn't cleared the air. If anything, it was even muggier than the day before.

Clouds were starting to pile up on the horizon and the atmosphere felt hot and heavy. Thunder grumbled in the distance. The rain wouldn't stay off for long. Maybe another shower would cool the air down a little. Neil felt hot and sticky in his costume. He could see Mrs Jones and Toby at the door of their cottage, trying to get some fresh air.

Neil went to his place by the drawbridge where the other extras were gathered. He greeted his friends and looked around him, still fascinated by the thrill of being part of an actual episode of *The Time Travellers*.

All the scenes recorded that day were going to be outside in the castle grounds.

There were four cameras set up, with thick cables trailing everywhere. One of the cameras was on the drawbridge itself, two on the lawn and one right on top of the battlements.

They were going to shoot the scene where Sir Gareth returned to his castle after years away. Neil looked up at the battlements. They would get a great aerial shot from there. Then he looked at Sir Gareth, waiting to ride into shot. What a pity he didn't have a Fred with him! It would have looked magnificent. Max was behind Sir Gareth on a little grey pony, and Prince was sitting patiently on the grass looking up at Max.

"Let's hope that dog gets it right first time," said a voice behind Neil. "It's going to rain soon."

Neil turned round. Mr Jenkins was standing behind him, his eyes on Prince.

"How long have you been a trainer, Mr Jenkins?" Neil seized this unexpected opportunity to find out more about the man's strange behaviour.

Jenkins looked suspicious. "What business is it of yours?"

Neil shrugged. "None, I suppose. Sorry. I'm

very interested in dogs, that's all. You don't seem to like them very much."

"Is that so? I've been training dogs for ten years now," said Mr Jenkins, briskly, rubbing his hand along his arm.

Neil bit his lip. "Oh. It's just—"

"You've got to show them who's boss," Jenkins cut in abruptly, "otherwise you just let yourself in for a lot of trouble." It was obvious from the tone of his voice that he didn't want to discuss the matter further.

Neil watched as Mr Jenkins turned and walked off.

"Quiet, everybody. Ready? Action!" shouted Brian.

Sir Gareth had started his ride across the lawn. Neil snapped to attention and watched Max follow on his pony with Prince trotting alongside. The extras turned to watch and point. Suddenly the grumbling thunder got louder. Neil saw Prince stop and turn back the way he had come. Sir Gareth's horse moved restlessly, pulling on the reins. Neil looked up. A great crack of lightning split the clouds and suddenly there was a loud roll of thunder.

"Cut!" shouted the director. "Will somebody get that dog out of shot!"

Neil caught a flash of movement out of the corner of his eye. Toby had jumped out of Mrs Jones's arms and was racing in terror across the lawn. Mrs Jones ran after him.

"Toby!" she called. "Come back here!"

But her voice was lost in another crack of thunder as lightning forked across the sky.

"Get everything under covers," Jeff Calton yelled, racing for the nearest shelter.

The first heavy drops of rain started to fall. Mrs Jones ran on, but by this time Toby was well ahead. Neil called the little dog's name. Sir Gareth's horse reared in terror as yet another flash of lightning lit the castle walls and thunder boomed from the battlements.

Toby was making straight for the horse. Prince lunged forwards, and started to bark furiously at Toby, warning the little dog away. Toby stopped, confused, as Prince ran towards him. Then, swerving, the little dog ran on towards the horse's flailing hoofs.

The rain began to fall in great driving sheets with stinging drops almost blinding Neil as he stood watching. Toby was barking frenziedly – nothing seemed to distract him.

Sir Gareth was still unaware of the impending danger and having trouble controlling his horse, which shuffled and stamped its enormous shaggy hoofs.

"No, Toby!" Neil yelled, running towards Toby just as the little dog was almost under the horse's hoofs.

Neil looked up. Sir Gareth pulled hard on the reins to try and regain control of the animal. The horse swerved and Neil threw himself at Toby, gathering up the terrified dog into his arms. Prince scampered out of harm's way as Max leapt down from his pony and ran to him.

Rain washed over Neil, running down his face, into his eyes, soaking him. He turned as he heard Mrs Jones cry out. She was stumbling blindly towards them.

"It's all right. I've got him," Neil called.

Mrs Jones tried to stop, but her feet slipped on the wet grass and she fell heavily.

Sir Gareth leapt off his horse and seized the reins, trying to lead the frightened animal away, but it pulled against him, pawing at the ground. The horse trainer ran up and grabbed the reins, steadying the animal.

Someone rushed past Neil. It was Jeff. He knelt down and cradled Mrs Jones' head in his arms. The old lady looked very white and her eyes were closed. Her right leg was bent under her at an impossible angle.

"Is she badly hurt?" Neil gasped.

Jeff looked up, his face streaming with water. "She's fainted. I think her leg might be broken. Take care of the dog. I'll see to Mrs Jones."

Brian ran up, a mobile phone in his hand.

"I'll call an ambulance," he shouted.

Behind him was a man with a huge umbrella. He opened it and held it over Jeff and Mrs Jones.

"Careful with that phone, Brian," Jeff said. "There's lightning around, remember."

Brian looked across the lawn to the open door of the cottage and thrust the mobile back in his pocket. "I'll phone from there. The first aider is on her way. We'll try to get Mrs Jones into the cottage if she can be moved." He ran off towards the house.

Mrs Wilson appeared, her face concerned. "Can I help?" she asked.

"Chris's mum is a nurse," Neil explained. "She's chaperoning us today."

The first aider arrived with the wardrobe mistress.

"A nurse?" she said to Mrs Wilson. "That's terrific."

Mrs Wilson bent over Mrs Jones, felt her pulse, and ran a hand gently over the twisted leg.

"I don't think it's safe to move her. We must be careful of that leg. We'll wait for the paramedics."

"OK. Everybody else into the castle," the wardrobe mistress told them briskly. "Come on, out of the rain. The costumes will be ruined."

Neil stood where he was for a moment, then he felt a tug on his arm.

It was Chris. "Come on, Neil. Mum will

66

look after Mrs Jones. Get Toby out of the rain!"

Neil looked down. The little dog was shivering violently in his arms.

"Sorry, Toby," he said as he followed Chris. "Let's get you inside. Where's Emily?"

"Already inside," Chris replied.

Neil looked back just as he reached the castle door. Toby was squirming in his arms, trying to get down, wanting his owner. Jeff and the first aider were shielding Mrs Jones from the rain with umbrellas. Mrs Wilson had covered her in blankets and looked as if she had everything under control.

"Not yet, Toby," Neil whispered, trying to calm the little animal. "You come with me. I'll look after you."

The great hall was full of people, standing in huddles, dripping water all over the floor. Neil saw Max taking some towels from one of the technicians and then looking around for the dogs.

"Bring Toby over here, Neil. I can dry Prince off with one of these. You can do the same."

Neil and Max pushed their way through the other actors and technicians towards the big chair in the middle of the hall. Chris left them to look for the others.

"Thanks," Neil said, taking one of the towels from Max's outstretched hand.

Neil and Max rubbed the dogs down until they were dry.

Neil looked at the cocker spaniel, still panting and enjoying all the attention from Max. "Prince is amazing. He was really excited by all the thunder and lightning, but he never really lost control, did he? I think he even enjoyed getting wet!"

Max smiled. "Nothing upsets Prince," he said. "He's got nerves of steel. I think he's used to all the bangs and flashes we put him through by now."

Toby was standing on the end of a table with his fur ruffled. He barked at Prince, wanting his new friend to play with him.

Max smiled. "What are you going to do with him?"

Neil frowned. He could hear the sound of an ambulance siren in the distance.

"I hadn't really thought about that," he said. "I suppose Mrs Jones will have to go to hospital." Then his face cleared. "But that's OK. I'll just take him home with me. He can stay at our kennels – he's been with us before."

"Kennels?" said Max.

"King Street Kennels, of course!" Chris Wilson appeared again beside him. "It's where Neil lives. The best hotel for dogs in Compton!"

Max opened his mouth to say something, but Neil had already turned away. The siren was louder now.

"I hope Mrs Jones is going to be OK." Neil looked thoughtful.

"If she is, it'll be no thanks to that dog!"

Everyone turned to see Mr Jenkins. Behind him, Jeff Calton was wiping his glasses on his wet shirt, trying to dry them off.

"What do you mean?" said Max, hotly.

"It was Prince that started it." Mr Jenkins was looking directly at Prince. "Why did he have to start barking like that? He scared the horse *and* that other dog."

Neil whirled round. "That isn't true. It was the thunder that scared the horse. If it hadn't been for Prince, Toby would have run right under the horse's hoofs."

Jenkins looked irritated. "So you say. But I know what I saw. And—"

"That's enough," said Jeff soothingly, running a hand through his hair. He looked at Neil. "Look, I know you caught Mrs Jones's little dog. And I'm grateful to you. But Mr Jenkins is the dog expert here."

Neil flushed. "Sorry," he mumbled. "But it wasn't the way Mr Jenkins said."

"I said, that's enough!" Jeff Calton's face was pale and he looked really worried. "This is all I needed right now. I'm just off to the hospital to see how Mrs Jones is. Brian will take care of things here. The plan was to finish up here today, but now we'll have to come back next week."

"Why can't we go on now?" asked Max.

Jeff frowned. "The place is a mire. The

equipment is going to have to be checked when the weather eases off. And, of course, we didn't get today's scenes done."

"You could do them tomorrow. We'll still be available – it's our half-term." Chris was desperate not to lose the opportunity to be in *The Time Travellers*.

Jeff shook his head. "Unfortunately, tomorrow is a bank holiday and the castle is booked for two days. We *can* pick up what we need to, but it'll be Wednesday before we can start shooting again. That means finding accommodation for the people who will have to stay and look after the equipment, redress the set, repair the damage – all that stuff. The actors have a couple of days off. Rats. We'd intended to be finished with Padsham today."

"When will *you* be back?" Max asked, anxiously.

"I'm going to Manchester after I've been to the hospital." Jeff Calton looked at Max. "Look, I know you like Prince, but this is getting out of hand. I'm going to see if I can get another dog."

Neil and Max were shocked.

"We've got several more episodes in the

series to shoot," Jeff continued, "and I need a dog I can rely on. Things just aren't working out with Prince any more, are they? I have to take Mr Jenkins' word on this matter."

Jeff Calton turned on his heel and walked off. Jenkins grunted then followed him. Neil turned to Max. The boy's face was white.

"It's not right," said Neil. "What Jenkins said wasn't true. Prince saved Toby's life."

Max buried his face in Prince's coat. "It's no good trying to tell them. I've tried millions of times. They won't listen."

"Why not? Why does Jeff listen to Jenkins all the time?" Neil was furious.

Max looked up. "You heard. We're just kids. Nobody listens to us. Jeff thinks *Jenkins* is the expert. He's always so busy getting the crew organized, he's blind to everything else. Face it, Neil. Prince won't be in the show any more. And if they won't let Prince do the show, I don't want to do it either."

# Chapter Six

"**W**hat? You're kidding, right?" Neil couldn't believe what he had just heard.

"I'm deadly serious." Max looked up. "I'm sick of being ignored."

Neil was shocked. He desperately thought about what he could do to make Max change his mind. He suddenly had a brilliant idea.

"I know somebody who will listen to us."

Max didn't react. "Who?" he asked, flatly.

Neil smiled. "My dad."

"Lucky you," said Max. "But what good does that do me?"

Neil thought for a moment. "I don't know,

but you could have a talk with Dad. I've already told him about Mr Jenkins."

"Do you really think Jeff would change his mind?" asked Chris.

Neil shrugged. "He might. But what's important is Prince. If Dad got a look at Prince he would be able to tell us what he thinks about him being spoilt. He runs obedience classes and can tell if a dog needs discipline like Mr Jenkins says."

"Prince doesn't," Max said firmly, giving the spaniel's ears a quick scratch. "He's so cool. Anyone can see that."

"Sticking up for Prince again, Max?" Brian Mason said, coming up to them.

"He's a good dog, Brian."

The director looked at Max and shook his head. "He's been giving us a lot of trouble on set lately."

"And we all know why," Max mumbled under his breath.

"Anyway, now we've got another problem with him."

"What now?" asked Max, impatiently.

"We're going to have to find somewhere for him to stay for the next few days."

Max's eyes suddenly lit up. "Neil's mum

and dad run a boarding kennels in Compton."

Brian looked at Neil. "Really? Do you think they could take Prince for a short while?"

"I *think* they could," Neil said, slowly. "I mean, we've got room. But I'd have to phone and ask them."

Brian dug in his pocket and brought out his mobile phone. "Go ahead. Tell them I'll bring Prince round right away if it's OK with them."

"When shall we leave?" asked Max, confidently.

Brian laughed. "*You'll* have to ask your chaperone, but I'm sure Suzie will let you. After all, we're finished here for the day, that's for sure." He shook his head. "I bet you'd be happy to spend the next few days in Prince's kennel with him, wouldn't you?"

Max laughed back at Brian. "I don't know about *in* the kennel, but I'd like to be with him." Suddenly he looked concerned. "Does this mean I can stay around too?"

"Ask your parents. You were due to go home for a couple of days," Brian said, thinking. "But if you wanted to stay and

Suzie was around, I suppose you could hang out here. A lot of the crew will be staying on."

"I'd like to stay. If Jeff gets a new dog I might never see Prince again. I'd like to be able to visit him at the kennels."

Neil looked at Max. The boy's hand was resting on Prince's head and his eyes looked as big and dark as the dog's. Max would really miss Prince. An idea began to form in Neil's mind.

Brian ran a hand through his hair. "And that's another thing I'll have to organize – accommodation for everybody." He looked at Neil. "If your parents could take Prince, it would be a load off my mind."

"I'll phone right now," Neil said. He looked at the little dog sitting by his feet. "I was going to ask them to take Toby anyway."

Brian grinned. "You must have really understanding parents."

"Oh, I do," Neil agreed, grinning. "Especially when it comes to dogs."

"Tell them we'll come round whenever they like." Brian disappeared to begin organizing the crew.

Neil nodded and punched the office number on Brian's mobile phone.

"Do you think they'll take Prince?" Max asked.

Neil nodded. "They've never refused yet." Then he grinned. "And I've had another idea."

"This sounds ominous!" Chris dug Max playfully in the ribs.

"What is it?" Max was anxious to find out.

"Wait and see," Neil laughed. Then he broke off. "Oh, hi, Mum. I've got a favour to ask."

"And these are the kennel blocks." Neil was leading the way across the courtyard at King Street Kennels. Brian, Suzie and Max were being shown round by Neil and his father.

Max looked around. "This is terrific! You're so lucky to live here, Neil. You'd be happy here, wouldn't you, Prince?"

The cocker spaniel looked up at him and wagged his tail. Toby trotted beside him. The little terrier had recovered from his fright.

"He'd have Toby for company," Bob Parker said. "Those two seem to get on really well."

"Oh, Dad, did Mum phone the hospital?" Neil asked.

Bob Parker nodded. "Mrs Jones has had her leg set, but she'll be in hospital for a couple of days, just to make sure everything is all right. I said I'd pop in later this evening."

"I'll look in too," Brian Mason, agreed. "I'll take her the biggest bunch of flowers I can find. I feel so guilty about her accident."

Neil was surprised. "It wasn't your fault. The grass was slippery from the rain."

"It's just that it happened on set," said Brian. "The company will pay for Toby's board as well as Prince's. That's the least we can do."

"I'm sure Mrs Jones will appreciate that," said Bob Parker.

Brian smiled. "You're a lifesaver, Bob," he said. "Now all I've got to do is confirm accommodation for the humans that need to stay on. In most cases I think I'll be able to extend the existing bookings."

"What about me?" asked Max. "I'd still really like to stay with Prince. We've only got a few days left."

Suzie put an arm round his shoulder. "Poor Max. We'll visit every day if the Parkers think that's OK."

"Hang on. I had an idea about that," said Neil, tripping over his words in his hurry to get them out. "I spoke to Mum and Dad about it when we got here. Max can stay with us if he likes. Then he'll be *really* close to Prince."

"Really?" Max's eyes were glowing. "With all these dogs? That would be so cool."

Bob Parker burst out laughing. "It'll mean bedding down in a sleeping bag on Neil's floor, but I don't suppose you'll mind that."

"You bet I won't. I'm not that stuck-up, you know!" He turned to Neil. "Cheers, mate."

Neil nodded. "No problem."

"You'll need permission, Max," Suzie chipped in. "You'll have to see what your parents have to say about it."

"Oh, Suzie, Mum and Dad will let me stay here if you tell them it's OK," Max said. "They've already said I can stop down here until we start shooting again."

Suzie grinned. "I'm sure you're right!"

"So everybody's happy?" Brian looked relieved. "You must feel like Santa Claus, Bob."

Bob Parker grinned. "I've got an ulterior motive. I'm going to get Max to help out with the kennel work."

"Really?" said Max, eagerly. "When can I start?"

# Chapter Seven

Next day Mrs Parker drove Max and Neil into Compton to see Mrs Jones in hospital. They had brought Toby and Prince along too.

"Are you sure it's all right to take the dogs?" Max asked as they drew up at the hospital.

Neil nodded. "The hospital has a pets visiting policy."

"I think it's a really good idea," Mrs Parker agreed. "Children get so attached to their pets, especially dogs. They make a much better recovery if they can see them sometimes."

"Mrs Jones is going to be so pleased to see

Toby," Neil said as he and Max clipped the leads on the dogs.

Mrs Jones *was* pleased. Her face lit up as they walked into the ward, and several of the other patients turned to admire the dogs.

Toby was straining at his lead to get to his mistress but Neil kept a tight hold.

"Hang on to him, Neil," Mrs Parker warned. "Pets visiting is one thing, but we can't have them running around!"

"So *this* is Toby," a nurse said as Toby reached Mrs Jones. "I've heard so much about the little chap."

"Meet Sister Williams," beamed Mrs Jones. "She's been so good to me."

The old lady was sitting in a chair by her bed with her leg propped up on a stool. She was surrounded by flowers. One huge vase was crammed with blooms. Brian Mason hadn't been joking when he said he'd get the biggest bunch he could find.

"Isn't he wonderful?" Mrs Jones looked so happy as Mrs Parker handed Toby to her. Toby's short stubby tail was waving madly as he reached up to lick Mrs Jones's face.

Mrs Jones's eyes were bright. "It's such a comfort to know he's at King Street."

"He loves it there," said Neil. "But I think he'd rather be with you."

Mrs Jones laughed as Toby tried to climb all over her.

"And there's Prince!" She reached down to stroke the cocker spaniel. "It was very thoughtful of you to bring him to see me,

Max. I hear you've had to stop recording *The Time Travellers* because of the storm."

A sudden flash of recognition crossed the nurse's face.

"I wondered where I'd seen you before. The children always gather round the TV when *The Time Travellers* is on. They think you're great – and Prince too!"

Max blushed. "Prince is the real star of the show."

Sister Williams glanced round towards the children's wing. "I wonder if you'd give the children a treat. They'd love a visit from you and Prince."

Max hesitated, then his face broke into a wide grin. "Sure. I'd love to. Lead the way!"

"Carole and I can have a nice long chat," Mrs Jones said, smiling at Mrs Parker.

Max and Neil followed Sister Williams out of the ward and down a short corridor.

"In here. This is the children's ward."

Neil looked around. The ward was brightly painted with pictures and posters on the walls. There were toys everywhere and a play area with a TV was down at the bottom of the ward. The little girl in the bed next to the door let out a shriek.

"It's Prince and Zeno! It's the time travellers!"

"It certainly is, Linda," Sister Williams said, smiling. "Let's go down to the play area and you can hear all about your favourite TV programme."

The children who were able to leave their beds gathered round, and soon Max was answering questions about the programme and giving autographs. Prince received a lot of attention too with everybody wanting to stroke and pat him.

"Oh, you're so lucky," said a little boy in a wheelchair. "I wish I had a dog like Prince."

"We could adopt Prince," Linda said suddenly. "He could be our mascot."

"You could send us pictures of him from all the different places you visit," said another child, excitedly.

Sister Williams smiled. "I don't know how Max would feel about that."

Max's face fell. "Sorry, but Prince won't be in the show any longer."

Neil could see that Max was upset.

"Why is that?" Sister Williams looked confused.

Max explained.

"But he's such a well-behaved dog," Sister Williams said, after hearing the story.

"They *can't* take him out of the show," said the little boy in the wheelchair. "It wouldn't be the same."

"I'm going to phone up the TV station and tell them not to sack Prince," Linda said, angrily.

Sister Williams laughed. "Calm down, Linda. You probably would do it, too!"

A quiet, dark-haired boy looked up. "We could all sign a petition. We'll tell them Prince is our mascot and we want him to stay in the show."

The other children cheered and nodded their agreement. "I'll go and get a pencil," Linda said. "We can start right now."

Sister Williams shook her head. "You've really given them something to think about now, Max." She looked at her watch. "It's nearly tea time. Maybe we should go back to Mrs Jones."

Max and Neil waved goodbye to the children. They were all in a huddle round Linda, trying to decide what to say in their petition.

"And Prince really is our mascot?" the little boy in the wheelchair called out.

Max nodded. "I'll send you a picture of him."

"And one of you," Linda added.

"OK." Max smiled. "And I'll bring Prince back again if I can."

"What *about* that?" said Neil as he and Max made their way back to Mrs Jones's ward. "You've got a fan club, Max."

Max shrugged. "Prince has."

"Do you really think they'll send a petition?"

Max shook his head. "Even if they did, what good would it do? You heard Jeff. He doesn't want to listen to kids."

"That's pretty daft for somebody who makes kids' TV programmes," Neil said, crossly. "Anyway, we haven't talked to Dad about it yet. We'll do that tonight."

"Has Prince ever shown signs of disobedience *before* coming to Padsham Castle?" Mr Parker asked later that evening.

Max shook his head. "He was great with his other trainer. It was just when Mr Jenkins came that he started acting up."

"So he *has* been acting up?" Mr Parker said, thoughtfully.

"A bit, I suppose," Max admitted. "But Mr Jenkins doesn't handle him properly. It sounds daft, but he seems nervous of Prince."

"It certainly *does* sound daft," Mr Parker agreed. He thought for a moment. "I tell you what. Let's get Kate to try Prince out tomorrow. Prince hasn't met Kate yet. She had a day off today and she was gone when you arrived back last night. She's a good dog handler and if Prince behaves for her the first time he meets her, then it isn't Prince we have to worry about."

"It's a deal," Max said, looking relieved. "But I just know it isn't Prince's fault."

"Down, boy," Kate said firmly. "Lie down."

Prince lay perfectly still while Kate walked across the courtyard. Sam came bounding out of the house to see what was going on. Neil made a move towards him, but his father put a hand on his arm.

"Leave it," Bob Parker said, quietly. "Let's see how Prince handles this."

The Border collie trotted over to Prince and barked. Neil watched Prince. The cocker spaniel's eyes were fixed on Kate. He didn't move a muscle, even when Sam nudged him on the flank.

"Sit!" Kate ordered.

Prince shifted to the sitting position in one fluid movement. His eyes were still on Kate.

Sam put his head on one side and wagged his tail. The tip of Sam's tail caught the other dog on the nose, but Prince still kept his eyes on Kate.

"Here, boy!" Kate called.

Prince leapt up excitedly.

"Walk!" said Kate.

Prince, instantly controlled, walked towards her.

She leant down and gave him a pat. "Good boy! Very good, Prince."

Prince wagged his tail as Kate stood up again. Sam barked. Prince looked up at Kate and she smiled.

"OK, Prince. Off you go!"

The two dogs raced off together across the courtyard.

Kate shrugged. "Perfect," she said as she came over to Mr Parker.

Bob Parker nodded. "That's what I thought. So now we know where the problem lies."

"With Jenkins," Max said angrily. "I knew it all along."

"It seems you were right," said Bob Parker. "But what exactly *is* his problem?"

Max shrugged. "I don't care what his problem is. All I know is that if we don't persuade Jeff that it isn't Prince's fault, then he's going to get rid of him."

"You could talk to him, couldn't you, Dad?"

Neil asked anxiously. "Convince him Jenkins is hiding something."

"I could." Bob Parker was thinking hard. "But I don't like to interfere, and if Prince has to work with Mr Jenkins, then we still have a problem."

"Time's running out, though," Max chipped in. "I know Jeff wants to start shooting at the castle again tomorrow. We've got to do something. We can't give up."

"Why don't we ask Jeff to give Prince one last chance?" suggested Neil.

Max shook his head. "It's no good. Prince won't work for Mr Jenkins."

"I wasn't thinking of him working with Mr Jenkins," Neil said slowly. "I was thinking of asking Jeff to try him out with a different trainer."

"Who?" said Max. "We haven't got another trainer."

Neil turned to Kate and smiled. "Yes, we have. A brilliant one. Kate!"

Max's face lit up and he looked pleadingly at the King Street kennel maid. "Kate?"

"But I've never done anything like that before." Kate was taken aback by the suggestion.

"You were great with Prince," Neil reasoned. "It might be our only chance."

Kate looked doubtful. "What do *you* think, Bob?"

"Jenkins isn't going to be too happy about it, that's for sure. But it might work," Mr Parker said.

Kate looked at Prince romping with Sam on the other side of the courtyard. Then she looked at Max.

"OK, I'll try."

Max threw his arms around Kate. "Thanks! Thanks a million."

"Don't thank me yet," Kate said, laughing. She shook her head until her ponytail bobbed. "What have I let myself in for?"

Neil grinned. "You can do it, Kate. I know you can do it."

# Chapter Eight

J eff Calton came round to King Street Kennels early on Wednesday morning to check that Max was fit and ready for the day's shooting ahead. He parked his car in the driveway and walked round to the back of the house. Everyone was in the kitchen eating toast.

The producer poked his head through the open door. "How's my star performer? Is he ready? You should be leaving soon."

Max crammed another piece of bread into his mouth and mumbled, "Nearly!"

"Have you found another Prince yet?"

Everyone looked at Sarah. She'd blurted

out what was on everyone's mind before anybody else had the chance.

Jeff Calton sighed. "Yes. The agency has come up with a couple of dogs they think might do."

"They'll never be as good as Prince," said Max, defensively.

The TV producer ran a hand through his hair. He looked stressed again. "Look, Max, I know how much Prince means to you, but I've got a deadline to meet. We've a long way to go in getting this episode recorded and we're already behind schedule. I just can't afford any more delays because Prince won't cooperate. Try to understand."

Max's mouth set in a stubborn line and Neil pushed his chair back and stood up.

"Can you give Prince just one more chance? He's fine now."

"He's had all the chances I can afford," Jeff said, shaking his head. "It's going to be a hectic day. We're going to pick up with the scene where Sir Gareth rides up to the castle."

Neil bit his lip. "It's still early though, isn't it?" he said.

Jeff nodded, looking puzzled.

"So we'll have time to bring Prince to the castle and let you see him rehearse a scene?" said Neil.

Max looked eagerly at Jeff. "That wouldn't hold you back much."

"I suppose not." Jeff sounded undecided. Then he sighed and shook his head. "It's a waste of time. Let it go, Max."

Max looked close to tears. Neil was disappointed too.

Jeff looked at Max, concerned. Then his face changed as he looked around and caught sight of Kate walking Fred across the courtyard towards them.

"Wow! What a magnificent dog!"

"That's Fred," said Neil proudly. "That's the Irish wolfhound I was telling you about."

Jeff suddenly seemed very interested. "Is that his owner?"

Max shook his head. "That's Kate, the kennel maid."

"She certainly knows how to handle a dog. Look how Fred is following her. He doesn't look in the least bit dangerous."

Neil looked. Fred was loping along beside Kate, his feet lifting high and head held steady, looking straight ahead.

Neil jumped in. "Kate is very good with dogs. She was going to bring Prince to the castle."

"So you had this all planned?"

Neil blushed but Jeff was thinking hard.

"You know that idea you had, Neil?"

"You mean about Sir Gareth having a war hound? I thought it would look great if Sir Gareth rode up to the castle with Fred trotting along beside him."

Then Jeff scratched his head. "I don't

suppose you know where I would find his owner, do you?"

Neil's mouth dropped open. "You mean you want to use him, after all? Mr Grey would be thrilled. I know he would."

"Grey," said Jeff, writing the name down on a scrap of paper. "And where can I find him?"

"I think he's coming to collect Fred this afternoon. Kate could tell you."

Jeff looked at them. "Wait here. And *don't* go away."

Max and Neil looked at each other.

"This could be really fantastic!" Neil said excitedly.

"And it could mean Jeff would give Prince one last chance. If he's in a good mood, there's still hope."

Neil watched as Jeff had a word with Kate. Then he saw the producer take his mobile phone out of his pocket and make a call. He spoke for a few moments, then handed the mobile to Kate. Kate spoke into the phone. She was nodding her head and obviously answering questions.

Jeff was grinning as he walked back towards the boys.

"Look, here's the deal. I've just been onto Mr Grey and he's agreed we can use Fred, so long as Kate comes with him. He'll meet us at the castle later." He paused and looked directly at Max. "Kate says she might as well bring both dogs along."

It took a moment for it to sink in.

"You mean Prince?" Max said.

Jeff nodded. "But don't go getting your hopes up, Max. If either of these other dogs from the agency is any good, I'll take it."

"You won't want to," said Max confidently. "Not after you've seen Prince again."

Jeff shook his head, laughing. "Talk about stubborn."

Neil's mouth was hanging open. "What made you change your mind?"

Jeff smiled. "I reckoned I owed you a favour. If your idea about using Fred works out, it's really going to add something special to one of the key scenes." His eyes took on a dreamy look. "I can see it now. I think we'll have the horses coming out of some mist. Then you'll see Fred. It'll be great. Brian will love it."

Jeff was still talking about the shot as he got into his car and drove away. Kate came towards them with Fred at her side.

Max turned to Neil. "It was you that changed his mind. Thanks for having that brilliant idea about Fred."

Neil grinned. "So now it's all systems go. C'mon, we've got to get ready. Keep your fingers crossed it'll all turn out OK." He rubbed Fred's ears. The big dog turned his head towards Neil's hand and his mouth lolled open. Fred loved the attention. "You're going to be a star, Fred – just like Prince. Isn't it great?"

Fred gave a friendly bark on cue and everyone laughed.

Kate tutted. "And now I'm taking two dogs instead of one. I must be mad."

"Mad about dogs," said Neil. "Like us!"

Kate drove Max, Neil and Emily over to Padsham Castle with the two dogs.

"I'm getting quite used to this." Neil jumped down from the Range Rover.

Emily looked around, then pointed towards the drawbridge. "There's Jeff. And Brian."

They were both talking to a couple of

cameramen as Brian lined up a shot of the drawbridge. Another man was close by, clutching a machine with a long tube.

"Put the mist machine over there," Brian said to him as Max and Neil ran up. "Make sure it's well out of shot. Where's the sound engineer? I need to talk to him."

Jeff turned just as Kate and Emily arrived with the dogs.

"Hi, you lot. Wow!" Brian gave Fred a friendly pat. "I'm really looking forward to seeing how this shot goes. We're getting the mist machine set up. You were right, Jeff. This *is* going to be something special. We'll be ready for the run-through in fifteen."

Fred raised his elegant muzzle and looked around him. The wolfhound wasn't in the least disturbed by all the activity. "What a dog!" Brian said before turning back to the cameramen.

Max hopped impatiently from foot to foot. "What about Prince?"

Jeff smiled. "Bring him over here out of Brian's way. We can try him out with a couple of moves. But, remember, I'm making no promises."

"What about trying the scene where I get

my cape caught on the drawbridge and Prince unhooks it?" said Max.

"OK," said Jeff. "Go and get into costume."

"I'd better go too," said Emily. "Are you coming, Neil?"

Neil shook his head. "I can slip mine on over my jeans and T-shirt. Can you collect it for me?"

Emily nodded and she and Max ran off to the wardrobe van. As they went, Neil saw a man approaching with two cocker spaniels.

"They look just like Prince!"

"That's the idea," said Jeff, raising his eyebrows. "I have to find a dog that looks exactly the same."

The man walked up to them. "Hi. I'm Phil Bolton. Where do you want me to show you the dogs?"

The producer looked round. "Here, if you like. There's a clear space just in front of the light rig." Then he turned to Kate and Neil. "Hang on a few more minutes, will you? I should see to these two first. Prince will have to wait a bit longer."

Neil and Kate exchanged anxious glances. Neil looked over at some of the light stands on the lawn. They stood about two metres high and had big flaps around the lights so that the beam could be directed where the cameras needed it. Cables trailed from them, snaking over the grass to one of the TV company's big generator vans.

"Can I watch?" asked Kate. "I'd like to see a real trainer at work. I might get some tips."

"I'm not really a trainer," the man said. "I thought *you* were the trainer."

Kate looked at Prince and Fred by her side. "Oh, no. I'm a kennel help."

"Our own trainer will be along any minute," said Jeff, looking at his watch. "He's a bit late this morning. At the moment all I want to see is if your dogs can obey basic commands."

Neil watched as the dogs were put through their paces and his heart quickly sank into his boots. The dogs behaved well – especially compared to Prince, who kept tugging at his lead, dragging on it and whining.

"Quiet, Prince," Kate said, firmly.

Jeff glanced across. "He still isn't behaving himself, is he?"

Kate shook her head. "I don't know what's got into him. He hasn't done this with me before."

Max rushed up, cape flying from his shoulders.

"That was quick," said Neil.

Max grinned. "I don't have to queue up!"

"Like the extras! Are Chris and Hasheem here yet?"

Max nodded. "Julie too. They're with Emily. Is Jeff ready to do the scene?" Then his face froze as he looked at the other two dogs. They looked like replicas of Prince and they were both behaving beautifully – coming to heel and sitting when told.

Prince barked and dragged his lead so hard Kate lost hold of it. At once Prince was off, round the back of the light stands, in amongst the wires and cables, barking furiously.

Jeff looked at him and shook his head. "There isn't any point trying him out. Look at him. He's out of control."

Neil and Max glared at Prince. He was standing, feet planted firmly on either side of a trailing wire, barking and howling.

Max was lost for words. "I don't

understand. I just don't understand."

"I do." Jeff's face was set like stone. "You can't say it's Mr Jenkins' fault now, can you, Max? He's not even here. Prince is finished. My only problem now is to decide which of these two dogs to choose."

# Chapter Nine

Neil was devastated. "Come on, Max. We might as well give up."

Max nodded dumbly and together the boys walked towards Prince. The cocker spaniel's barking grew even more frenzied but, when Max put a hand on his collar, he wouldn't move.

Even Max began losing patience with the dog. "Come on, Prince!"

Neil was looking intently at Prince. "Wait a minute. *Why* won't he move?"

"Because Jeff is right, Neil. He won't do as he's told."

"That isn't true, though. We know that. He was fine this morning. And look at

Fred, he's not moving a muscle!"

The big shaggy dog was calm, unmoved by the noise Prince was making.

Neil got down beside Prince and put a hand on his neck. "What is it, boy? What's wrong?"

Kate and Max looked on, anxiously.

Neil's other hand brushed a cable at his feet and he drew it back sharply. "Ouch!"

"What?" said Max.

"The cable's hot," gasped Neil. As he looked at the cable, a thin wisp of smoke rose from it. "It's smouldering," Neil said. "It's on fire."

Then Jeff heard him. "What was that? Get out of there, Neil. Right away!"

"Prince won't budge," said Neil.

But Jeff was already yelling to a runner. "Get a sparky, someone. We need a technician straight away! And pull the plug on this light stand. Hurry, man!"

The runner tore off towards one of the vans. Seconds later another man in blue overalls came hurtling out of the van and was down on his knees beside the cable.

Max and Neil dragged Prince away and tried to settle him down next to where Fred was sitting. Prince kept barking at the man beside the cable.

Jeff's face was white. "What's up?"

The technician looked up. "It looks like a short circuit. Keep everybody away while I get it sorted out."

"Is it fixable?"

"Just about. I'll have to rewire the whole stand. It looks as if the wires are slow burning inside the casing. It was only a matter of time before the casing burnt through. Anybody who had touched it would have been in real trouble."

"Electrocuted?" Jeff looked appalled.

Already a crowd had started to gather. Chris and Hasheem had heard the commotion and came running up. Julie and Emily were close on their heels. They were already in costume.

"What's going on?" asked Emily, concerned.

Neil filled her in. "There's something wrong with the lights. They could have blown up."

"Keep back," Jeff warned. He turned to Max. "Thank goodness Prince started playing up."

"Wait a minute," said the man with the two

cocker spaniels. "I think it was a bit more than that."

"What do you mean?" Jeff sounded surprised.

"It looks to me as if Prince smelt the cable burning."

Max jumped in. "He was warning us. I told you Prince was clever."

Jeff's mouth gaped open. "Well, if that's true, I certainly owe him an apology."

"If the light had blown, it would have been a disaster!" Neil gasped.

"Somebody might have been *hurt* . . ." said Jeff, looking worried.

"You see, he *wasn't* misbehaving," pleaded Max. "Give him another try, please, Jeff."

The big wolfhound barked twice as if in agreement.

Chris coughed to get everybody's attention, then he looked at Jeff. "I've got something for you. My mum was at the hospital today. Mrs Jones is coming home tomorrow."

"That's great." Jeff smiled.

"The sister on the children's ward gave Mum this. It's for you."

Chris held out a pink envelope with a picture of some elephants on it.

Jeff looked at the envelope in disbelief. "Elephants? Er, are you sure this is for me?"

Chris nodded. "Positive."

Jeff opened the envelope and took out several sheets of paper. They seemed to be covered in names. The producer ran a hand through his hair and laughed. "Well, I never."

"What?" said Max.

"You know what this is?" Jeff asked.

Max shook his head.

"It's a petition from the children's ward at the hospital. You've got them all on your side, Max."

"Everybody likes Prince. He's OK. I've been trying to tell you that. Nobody wants to see him go."

"So I can see! Well, maybe we *will* have to give Prince that trial after all."

"*Yes!*" said Max, punching the air. "I'll go and set things up on the drawbridge. You tell Kate what she has to do. And don't be long!"

Neil watched as Max ran towards the castle.

"Here," said Kate, handing Fred's lead to Neil. "Wish me luck."

"Jenkins hasn't shown up yet, so I'll take you through things myself. Now what Prince has to do is . . ." Jeff began, walking across the lawn with Kate and Prince. The dog walked calmly at Kate's heels.

"What was all that about?" asked Hasheem, scratching his head. He bent down and ruffled Fred's ears.

Neil explained while they watched Prince go through the scene. It was perfect. The cocker spaniel had to run across the drawbridge in front of Max, then Max fell and his cape got caught. Prince had to run back and free him.

"Look at that," said the man with the

spaniels. "It would take my dogs ages to learn to do that."

Max came racing across the grass to them with Prince in hot pursuit. "Perfect!" he cried.

Neil nodded. "Great stuff, Max. And well done, Prince!"

"But can we be sure he'll be reliable?" said Jeff, a moment later as he reached them.

"He was reliable with me," Kate confirmed.

Jeff still looked worried. He looked up. "Here's Harry Jenkins. Let's see what he thinks."

Jenkins was coming in through the castle gates. He walked slowly across the lawn towards them. His eyes were fixed on Fred. Neil stared at him and followed his eyes. The man seemed transfixed by the sight of the wolfhound.

There was a shout from the castle gates. A short, stocky man was hurrying through them behind Jenkins. Fred started forward and barked once. Then the dog looked up at Neil.

"It's Mr Grey," said Kate. "Fred's owner."

Neil bent down to Fred and unclipped his lead. "Go on, boy," he whispered. "Go to your master."

The huge wolfhound leapt forward and began to run in great loping strides towards his master – and towards Harry Jenkins.

The dog trainer immediately put his arms up in front of his face. "Get it away from me," he yelled. "Call that dog off!"

Fred hesitated a moment, then continued towards his owner, straight past Jenkins.

Neil looked at the terrified man, staggering towards them. The trainer turned and dropped his arms. His face was chalk white.

"What on earth is the matter?" Jeff said, running up to him. "Are you ill or something? The dog was nowhere near you. It was running past you, man."

Jenkins gritted his teeth. "I thought it was going for me."

Jeff's eyes narrowed. "You were scared by a dog? But you're a dog *trainer*!"

Jenkins nodded and didn't look at anybody. Neil noticed that he was rubbing his arm again. Neil had seen him do that before.

Jeff probed further. "You stepped in to cover on *The Time Travellers* because I thought you were one of the best dog trainers around. I trusted your judgement!"

"I *used* to be one of the best," Harry Jenkins said, guiltily. He had the look on his face of a man who had just been found out.

"What do you mean?"

"I was very badly bitten on the arm by an Alsatian a couple of months ago. It got to me. This is my first job since. I thought I would be OK with a cocker spaniel."

"But you clearly aren't, are you?" Jeff was obviously furious.

Jenkins shook his head. "I was coming to tell you anyway. I've been ill this morning just thinking about it. I don't think I can do the show any longer."

Neil and Max exchanged unbelieving looks.

Max wanted answers too. "You kept blaming Prince, Mr Jenkins."

The man looked thoroughly miserable. "I know. I'm sorry. A dog senses when a trainer is nervous. I should have known. It isn't Prince's fault. It's mine. I've handled everything so badly."

Jeff was furious. "I don't believe it! This is just what I need right now."

Neil swallowed. He was beginning to feel sorry for the trainer. "Look, Mr Jenkins. Just because one dog bit you, that doesn't mean it's going to happen again. I mean, I'm sure you could do *something* about getting your confidence back."

Jenkins nodded. "I know. I'm thinking things through now. But I need time-out regardless. You'll need to find another trainer, Jeff."

"You should have told me," Jeff said, stonily. "I can't be expected to do everybody's job as well as mine."

"I'm sorry." Jenkins turned away and began to walk back towards the castle gate. As he passed Max and Prince he gave a weak smile and patted the golden cocker spaniel affectionately on the head. Then he left.

Max laid a hand on the producer's arm. He'd softened a little bit. "I feel a bit sorry for Mr Jenkins. I mean, it was quite brave of him to carry on working with Prince when he was feeling so uncomfortable, wasn't it?"

"I suppose so." Jeff shook his head. "And it was you who kept saying it wasn't Prince's fault. You're the one who should be feeling hard done by."

"I'm not angry. I'm just glad Prince has got his job back."

"Prince is saved!" Chris patted Max on the

back and Hasheem joined in. As Neil and Kate congratulated Max too, shaking him energetically by the hand, Prince's tail thumped on the grass. He knew everyone was happy and he was determined to join in.

"Speaking of jobs," said Jeff, interrupting the celebrations. "I could use another trainer." He turned to Kate. "I don't suppose you want a job with a TV production company, do you, Kate?"

Neil held his breath. Kate would never leave King Street Kennels, would she?

Kate laughed. "I've *got* a job," she said. "A job that I love." She winked at Neil. "I wouldn't leave King Street for anything. But I'll help you out this afternoon. How's that?"

"Great," said Jeff, grinning. "Now, let's introduce Fred to Sir Gareth. This is going to be a great shot! Brian is really excited about it."

Kate went to meet Mr Grey. Fred was obviously overjoyed to see his master again and poor Mr Grey was having a hard time keeping his feet while Fred put his front paws on the little man's shoulders. Neil hoped Kate could get Fred calm enough for the shoot. Somehow, he knew she would.

Neil turned to watch as Jeff set off with a determined walk towards the drawbridge. Brian Mason was standing by, conducting the cast and crew, waving his hands in the air and talking to three people at once – about different things!

The man with the cocker spaniels looked at Neil. "I guess that's me done. I'd better get back."

Neil bit his lip. "It isn't that there's anything wrong with your dogs, Mr Bolton," he said, bending down to stroke the spaniels' floppy ears.

"I know that," said the man. "They've been in tons of adverts and TV dramas before. But to tell the truth, these two are twins and they hate being apart. So maybe it's for the best."

"Maybe it is," said Neil as the two dogs licked his face.

He could hear Brian shouting in the distance. "Get that mist machine going! Where's Sir Gareth? Max, get on that pony! Extras! Where is my crowd? Come on! We haven't got all day. Good boy, Prince! Thank goodness somebody knows what they're doing around here!"

Neil ran towards the wardrobe van and scrambled into his costume. Kate was already at the drawbridge, leading Fred to stand beside Sir Gareth's horse. Mr Grey was standing some way off, watching proudly.

Chris waved at Neil. "Come on!"

Brian was still shouting. His voice rebounded off the castle walls as Neil skidded into place beside Emily and the others.

"Ready, Sir Gareth? Kate, Fred looks wonderful! Start the mist – and – action!"

# Chapter Ten

*Sir Gareth rode out of the mist, his faithful war hound loping along beside him. Behind him, on a small grey pony, rode Zeno, with Prince at his side. The castle loomed out of the swirling mist and, at a window in the topmost tower, a face appeared. It was the Lady Genevieve, imprisoned by the wicked Baron Dredmore.*

*The riders reined in their mounts and Prince let out a sharp bark. At once the ground was alive with figures, appearing from nowhere out of the mist, gathering silently around the riders.*

*Sir Gareth raised his lance and pointed to the drawbridge. The villagers closed in behind the riders as Sir Gareth and Zeno rode their horses across the bridge. A cry of warning went up from the castle but it was too late. The villagers raised their voices in a great roar of triumph and charged!*

"Wow!" Neil whispered. "It *does* look great."

"There *we* are!" Chris was pointing at the large screen in his excitement.

"Oh, look!" Emily cried. "Isn't it weird seeing yourself on TV?"

The little preview suite at Prince Productions in Manchester was crammed to bursting point. As well as Max and all the rest of the actors, there were some of the extras from Meadowbank School, Max's parents, Bob and Carole Parker and Sarah, Mr Grey and, of course, Mrs Jones. The dogs were there too – including Toby, who got quite excited when he saw Prince on the screen.

"Down with Baron Dredmore!" yelled the extras on screen and Neil was tempted to join in.

There were also a few special guests of honour. Jeff had invited some of the children who'd been in Compton Hospital. Sister

Williams came too – and she was just as excited.

The time tunnel appeared on screen and Zeno and Prince disappeared into it. The theme music played and the titles rolled. The lights came up and everybody sat back.

"That was great!" said Julie, excitedly.

"It was brilliant!" agreed Hasheem. "I'm definitely going to be an actor when I grow up."

"You already *are* an actor," mocked Chris. "At least, according to Mr Hamley."

Jeff stood up in the front row and faced the audience. "Well, I hope you all enjoyed that!"

The room suddenly erupted with a loud chorus of shouts and cheers.

"Don't forget that there's food laid out next door, everybody," Jeff said when everyone was finally quiet again.

Chris grinned. "Great! I'm starving."

"First though, I've got a few people to thank," Jeff went on. "Most importantly, King Street Kennels. If it hadn't been for King Street, and especially Neil, Prince might have been out of a job and we'd have lost a really great doggy star."

"Hear! Hear!" Max yelled. "Let's hear it for King Street and the Puppy Patrol!"

There was more loud cheering and Jeff had to raise his voice to make himself heard. "Then there's Kate and Fred."

Neil turned round and smiled at Kate and Mr Grey. Fred was sitting between them.

"Imagine my Fred being a star," said Mr Grey, proudly. "I'm going to get a photograph from Prince Productions to put up in the shop."

"A framed photograph," said Jeff, laughing. "And if I ever need an Irish wolfhound again . . ."

"You just come to me and Fred," said Mr Grey, laying a hand on the wolfhound's shaggy head.

Fred looked up at him and Neil smiled.

"I'm also keeping Toby in mind," Jeff said, pointing to the old lady and her little dog in the fifth row.

Mrs Jones laughed. "I don't think my Toby's got star quality. But he suits me!"

Jeff had sent a car for Mrs Jones. She still had to use crutches, but her leg was on the mend.

"There's one more announcement," said

Jeff above the laughter. "But I think I'll let Brian make that one since the person who thought it up is too shy to do it."

Brian leapt to his feet and stood beside Jeff. He was holding a piece of pink paper in his hand. "This is the petition from the children at the hospital."

Emily cheered and the children joined in.

"Jeff and I are going to keep this," Brian went on. "In fact we're going to put it on our office wall – just to remind us that we should always listen to what *The Time Travellers'* fans say."

"I'm for that," Julie shouted out, then blushed.

"And we're going to have the biggest fund-raiser ever for the children's ward at Compton. There's going to be a summer fun day out at Padsham Castle in aid of the hospital – with the stars of all your favourite TV programmes. You'll be very impressed when you see the line-up we've got for you."

"Brilliant!" Neil laughed and turned to Max. "That was a great idea."

Max's jaw dropped. "How did you know it was *my* idea?"

Neil gave him a shove. "Don't be daft," he

said. "It's exactly the kind of thing you'd think of. You're a star!"

Max shook his head and looked around. "Not me! It was you and the hospital and Kate and all the rest who really cared that saved Prince. You're the stars."

"And so is Prince," added Neil.

"Oh, definitely. Prince is a star all right, aren't you, boy?"

Prince looked up and thumped his tail on the floor.

A tall man with dark hair stood up. "I've also got something to say," he said.

"Dad?" said Max, puzzled. Max's dad smiled at him, then turned to face the other, expectant faces. "I've got a surprise for Max. His mum and I didn't realize just how fond he was of Prince."

Neil looked at the woman sitting next to Max. She smiled at her son as he looked enquiringly at her.

"What's going on?" mouthed Max.

"Wait and see," his mum whispered.

"To cut a long story short," Max's dad continued. "We've been in touch with the animal agency – and they're going to *sell* Prince. To Max."

Max's mouth hung open. He looked too shocked to speak.

"Well, say something," said his mum, with a wide grin.

Max looked at his parents, then at Prince.

"Mine?" Max couldn't believe it. "Prince is really mine?"

Prince looked up at him and barked. Max put his arms round the cocker spaniel's neck.

"Did you hear that, Prince?" he said. "Now we'll always be together."

Neil looked at Max's parents. "I think he's pleased."

Everybody laughed.

"Food, anybody?" said Brian.

There was a cheer and a mad rush for the door – dogs as well as children.

After all, Neil thought, looking at Max and Prince – even stars have to eat!

# Puppy Patrol titles available from Macmillan Children's Books

The prices shown below are correct at the time of going to press. However, Macmillan Publishers reserve the right to show new retail prices on covers which may differ from those previously advertised.

| 1. Teacher's Pet | Jenny Dale | £2.99 |
| 2. Big Ben | Jenny Dale | £2.99 |
| 3. Abandoned! | Jenny Dale | £2.99 |
| 4. Double Trouble | Jenny Dale | £2.99 |
| 5. Star Paws | Jenny Dale | £2.99 |
| 6. Tug of Love | Jenny Dale | £2.99 |

All Macmillan titles can be ordered at your local bookshop or are available by post from:

**Book Service by Post
PO Box 29, Douglas, Isle of Man IM99 1BQ**

Credit cards accepted. For details:
Telephone: 01624 675137
Fax: 01624 670923
E-mail: bookshop@enterprise.net

**Free postage and packing in the UK.**
Overseas customers: add £1 per book (paperback)
and £3 per book (hardback).